THE SPLENDID BELT OF MR. BIG

The
Splendid
Belt
of
Mr. Big

Sara Bulette

ILLUSTRATED BY LOU MYERS

Reading Consultant: Morton Botel

 Follett Publishing Company
Chicago   New York

Library of Congress Catalog Card Number: 64-10360

SECOND PRINTING   L/T/A 8230

Mr. Big was sad.

"I am too big," he said.

"I can't get a belt to fit me."

Mrs. Big said, "Make a belt."

Mr. Big did make a belt.
"It will fit my middle.
It is a splendid belt," he said.
Mrs. Big said, "Yes, it is.
Splendid belts will sell well.
You can make belts to sell."

"I will," said Mr. Big.
"I will make little belts.
And I will make big belts."

Mrs. Big said, "No belt will be
as splendid as your belt."

Mr. Big made little belts.

He made big belts.

And he hung the belts on his neck.

"I will sell my belts," said Mr. Big.
"Sell the belts," said Mrs. Big.
"But do not sell your splendid belt.
Do not sell the belt that fits you."

Off went Mr. Big.
He sang, "Belts to sell!
Belts to sell!
Splendid
big and little
belts to sell!"

Mr. Big went past the zoo.
"I must rest," he said.
And he did.

Mr. Big looked at the monkeys.

And the monkeys looked at Mr. Big.

Mr. Big went *clap! clap!*

And the monkeys went *clap! clap!*

"Ho! Ho! Ho!" said Mr. Big.

"Monkey see, monkey do!"

"Ho-hum!" said Mr. Big.

"I will nap."

He hung up the belts.

And he had a nap.

"See! See! See!" said the monkeys.

Mr. Big sat up. He looked.

The little monkeys had the little belts.

The big monkeys had the big belts.

Mr. Big shook his fist.

"Give me my belts!" he said.

"Give me my little belts.

And give me my big belts!"

17

A little monkey shook his fist.
He said, "See! See! See!"
A big monkey shook his fist.
He said, "See! See! See!"

Mr. Big clapped his hands.

The monkeys clapped, too.

"See! See! See!" said the monkeys.

"Ho! Ho! Ho!" said Mr. Big.
"Monkey see, monkey do!
I can get my belts."
　　Mr. Big took off his big belt.

The monkeys took off the belts.

Mr. Big ran to get the belts.

He hung the belts on his neck.

He put on his splendid belt.

And off he went.

He sang, "Belts to sell!

Belts to sell!

Splendid

big and little

belts to sell!"

The little lads came to see Mr. Big.

The big men came to see Mr. Big.

"Ha! Ha! Ha!" said the little lads.
"Mr. Big has belts on his neck."
"Ho! Ho! Ho!" said Mr. Big.
"This little belt will fit you."
And the lads got the little belts.

"Big belts to sell," said Mr. Big.
"Splendid big belts to sell."

The big men said, "Ha! Ha! Ha!"

Mr. Big said, "Ho! Ho! Ho!
This big belt will fit you."

And the big men got the big belts.

Back went Mr. Big to his house.

"Did you sell the belts you made?" said Mrs. Big.

"Yes, the big belts and little belts.

"But not my splendid belt.
Not the splendid belt of Mr. Big!"

THE SPLENDID BELT OF MR. BIG

Reading Level: Level One. *The Splendid Belt of Mr. Big* has a total vocabulary of 82 words.

Uses of This Book: Reading for fun. Children will enjoy the story of Mr. Big, who makes splendid belts. And they will be amused by his adventure when he tries to sell the belts.

Word List

All of the 82 words used in *The Splendid Belt of Mr. Big* are listed. Regular plurals (-*s*) and regular verb forms (-*s*, -*ed*, -*ing*) of words already on the list are not listed separately, but the endings are given in parentheses after the word.

7	Mr.		belt(s)		is
	big		to		splendid
	was		fit		yes
	sad		me		sell
	I		Mrs.		well
	am		make		you
	too				can
	he	8	did		
	said		it	9	little
	can't		will		and
	get		my		no
	a		middle		be

	as		must	19	clapped
	your		rest		hands
10	made	14	looked	20	took
	hung		at		
	the		monkey(s)	21	ran
	on		clap		put
	his		ho		
	neck		see	22	lads
					came
11	but	15	ho-hum		men
	do		nap		
	not		up	23	ha
	that		had		has
					this
12	off	16	sat		got
	went				
	sang	17	shook	25	back
			fist		house
13	past		give		
	zoo			26	of

The Follett BEGINNING-TO-READ Books

Purpose of the Beginning-to-Read Books: To provide easy-to-read materials that will appeal to the interests of primary children. Careful attention is given to vocabulary load and sentence length, but the first criterion is interest to children.

Reading Levels: These books are written at three reading levels, indicated by one, two, or three dots beneath the *Beginning-to-Read* symbol on the back cover. *Level One* books can be read by first grade children in the last half of the school year. As children increase their reading ability they will be able to enjoy *Level Two* books. And as they grow further in their reading ability they will progress to *Level Three* books. Some first grade children will read *Level Two* and *Level Three* books. Many third graders, and even some fourth graders, will read and enjoy *Level One* and *Level Two* books, as well as *Level Three* books. The range of interest of *Beginning-to-Read* books stretches far beyond their reading level.

Use of the Beginning-to-Read Books: Because of their high interest and readability, these books are ideal for independent reading by primary children—at school, in the library, and at home. The books may also be incorporated into the basic reading program to develop children's interests, expand their vocabularies, and improve word-attack skills. It has been suggested that they might serve as the foundation for a skillfully directed reading program. Many *Beginning-to-Read* books correlate with the social studies, science, and other subject fields. All will help children grow in the language arts. Children will read the *Beginning-to-Read* books with confidence, with success, and with real enjoyment.

30